*For Gwenny, who helped me
grow into a big bear and will
always be in my heart*

Copyright © Ella Burfoot, 2006
The rights of Ella Burfoot to be identified as the author and illustrator of this work
have been asserted by her in accordance with the Copyright, Designs and Patents Act, 1988.
First published in Great Britain in 2006 by Andersen Press Ltd, 20 Vauxhall Bridge Road,
London SW1V 2SA. Published in Australia by Random House Australia Pty.,
20 Alfred Street, Milsons Point, Sydney, NSW 2061. All rights reserved.
Colour separated in Switzerland by Photolitho AG, Zürich.
Printed and bound in Singapore.

10   9   8   7   6   5   4   3   2   1

British Library Cataloguing in Publication Data available.

ISBN-10: 1 84270 485 0
ISBN-13: 978 1 84270 485 1

This book has been printed on acid-free paper

BEAR
AND
ME

Ella Burfoot

Andersen Press • London

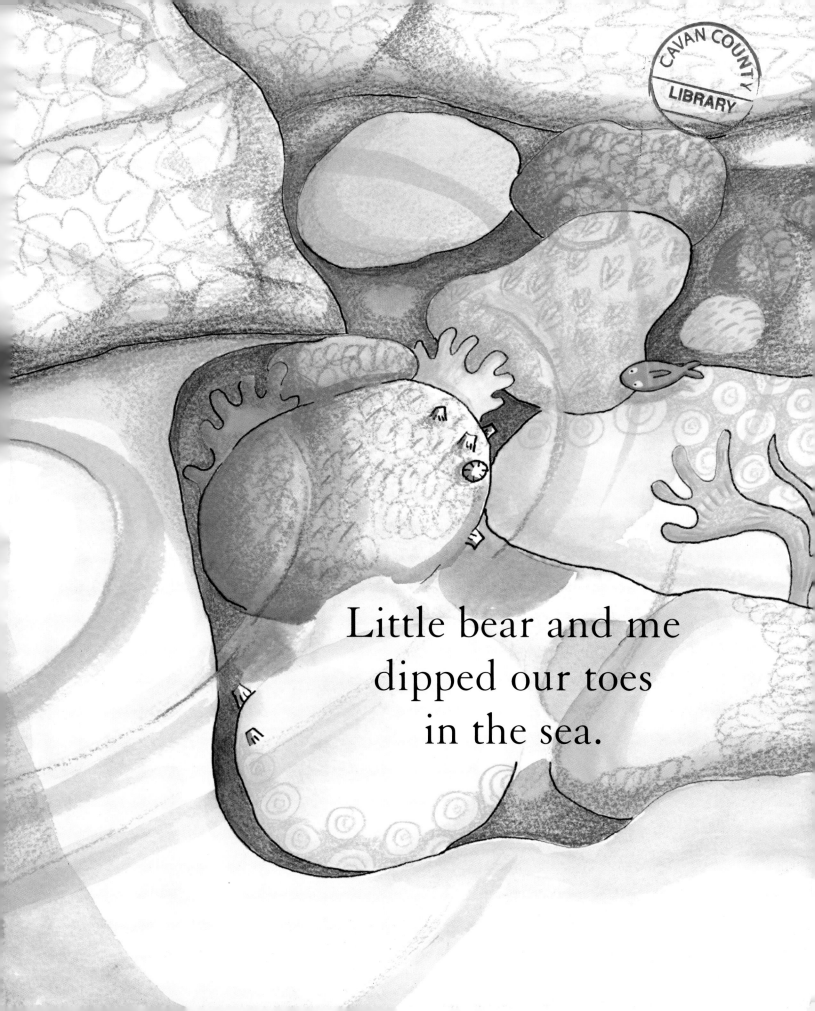

Little bear and me
dipped our toes
in the sea.

We dipped our toes,
but we didn't go in ...

because little bear can't swim.

Little bear and I
looked up at the sky.

We didn't get on the plane,
just looked up at the sky ...

because little
bear says he
can't fly.

Me and little bear
sat on the stair.

Sitting there
was just fine ...

because little bear doesn't like to climb.
I told little bear that it was quite O.K.,

because I know that one day . . .

he'll be a big bear
and not so scared.

And then
we'll swim …

and climb . . .

and fly . . .

that big bear and I.

Other paperback picture books to enjoy:

Burger Boy
by Mei Matsuoka and Alan Durant

Misery Moo
by Jeanne Willis and Tony Ross

Norman's Ark
by Michael Foreman

Will and Squill
by Emma Chichester Clark